Making Reading Fun!

Chrysalis Children's Books

I wanted to write my new address here but mummy didn't give me the address yet.

Mum is driving me to school.

Granny bakes cakes for us.

I like her, she has 2 cats.

I like Mrs Larsson, she is nice.

This is my diary.

Daddy with the boxes.

First published in Great Britain in 2005 by
Chrysalis Children's Books
an imprint of Chrysalis Books Group plc
The Chrysalis Building, Bramley Road, London W10 6SP
www.chrysalisbooks.co.uk

A CIP catalogue record for this book is available
from the British Library.

ISBN 1 84458 375 9

Printed in China

2 4 6 8 10 9 7 5 3 1

This book can be ordered direct from the publisher.
Please contact the Marketing Department.
But try your bookshop first.

Hello my name is Louis and this is my room.

Bobo usually sleeps right next to me. He is my dog.

← my desk! (For doing homework and drawing.)

Louis

Last week, I had a ~~fairwell~~ farewell party at school. Mrs Larsson, our teacher, gave me a book about dogs.

M N O P Q R S T U V X Y

This is for you, Louis!

STOP PICKING YOUR NOSE, PHILIP.

Leave me alone!

I don't know where we are moving to, but I'll be going to a new school.

I won't see Grandma every day then.

Bobo was due for a walk.
But first, Mummy gave us a
key on a seahorse key chain.
She said,

"Put it into your
little bag,
Louis!"

On our walk,
Bobo and I invented a
great game!

He was a special
secret agent
and had to find me me.

(Only by the
smell of my glove!)

5

4

3

I said,
"Bobo count to 10 (ten)
and then go find me!"

1

2

But instead,
he was talking
to the cat...

This is
my other
watch.

8:20

7.

6

and I had
to wait
for ages!

9

10

I don't know what is wrong with Bobo sometimes.

He ate my spare watch. →
This is all that's left of it!

Daddy was waiting for us. And he was in a bit of a rush.

Dad said,

"It's getting late and it's going to snow soon! This is the worst time of the year to be moving anyway."

"I don't want to move at all," I said.

"Bye bye house, bye bye street!"

SOLD

770-1

TWIT TWOO!

I went off to play with Bobo in the garden.

It was a bit strange there.

The strange girl in the tree said, "I'm Jackie! Do you want to meet my tortoise Priscilla?"

Jackie lived right next door (no. 23) and her mum invited us in for a cup of tea.

Jackie had a great idea.

Priscilla!

BObo!

We timed how fast Priscilla and Bobo made it from the living room into the Kitchen when we called them.

I know why Bobo was so fast!
(He'd smelled my cookies again.)
The tortoise didn't arrive at all!
00:06
08.12
P

It was already bedtime for Priscilla when the van finally arived.

But for tomorrow,
Mum invited everyone to
our new home.
That was great, because
I knew she'd bought a
chocolate cake for us!

I like Jackie.
Jackie is really good at drawing.

Hi Louis!

Cake!

This is Jackie's tortoise.

This cat lives at our place somewhere.

(Jackie wrote this.)

Jackie

Jackie lives at number 23.

Our new house.

No. 25

Me + Bobo.

Bone

More fun books for you to read!

ISBN 1 84365 056 8

ISBN 1 84365 061 4

ISBN 1 84458 140 3 (pb)

ISBN 1 84365 026 6 (hb)
ISBN 1 84458 157 8 (pb)

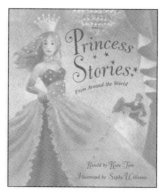

ISBN 1 84365 025 8

ISBN 1 84365 017 7